Once Upon Yesterday

Naomi Noon

Outskirts Press, Inc.
Denver, Colorado

This is a work of fiction. The events and characters described herein are imaginary and are not intended to refer to specific places or living persons. The opinions expressed in this manuscript are solely the opinions of the author and do not represent the opinions or thoughts of the publisher. The author has represented and warranted full ownership and/or legal right to publish all the materials in this book.

Once Upon Yesterday
All Rights Reserved.
Copyright © 2009 Naomi Noon
V1.0

This book may not be reproduced, transmitted, or stored in whole or in part by any means, including graphic, electronic, or mechanical without the express written consent of the publisher except in the case of brief quotations embodied in critical articles and reviews.

Outskirts Press, Inc.
http://www.outskirtspress.com

ISBN: 978-1-4327-3820-4

Library of Congress Control Number: 2008943045

Outskirts Press and the "OP" logo are trademarks belonging to Outskirts Press, Inc.

PRINTED IN THE UNITED STATES OF AMERICA

I dedicate this book to the memory of my parents who did the best they could for me

CHAPTER 1

The day of February 1955 on which Yolanda Yee started at the School of Architecture was a typical summer day in Sao Paolo, she could tell it was going to be a beautiful day. When she left home at six o'clock in the morning, the sun had already broken the pale sky and was emitting yellow, golden and orange shines at the horizon. The breeze was barely perceptible and the morning air was fresh and crisp.

When she arrived at the School of Architecture at a little after eight o'clock, the sun had risen and hung like a halo in mid-sky emitting eye-blinding rays. The breeze had died down and the still air was mildly warm on her skin.

The School of Architecture used to be the residence of a philanthropist who donated the property to the university to be the school. It was in another part of town, far from the main campus of the university, in a quiet residential neighborhood of old mansions, tree lined streets, and sidewalks paved with white mosaic and inlays of black mosaic in exquisite geometric patterns.

The fence along the south at the front of the property was made of eight-foot black iron bars with spearhead shaped tips. From the double leaved gate in the middle of the fence, an eight-foot wide footpath extended to an eight-foot wide stair that rose from the foot of the Mansion to an eight-foot square platform on the first floor outside the front entrance to the Mansion. The footpath, the stair, and the platform were paved with broken flagstones; and the sides of the platform and the stair were guarded by bulky parapets of rough stone that curved out at the foot of the stair to form into two giant round piers on the ground. The footpath split the front yard into two lush lawns with mature and shady trees scattered on them; and under each tree, there was a black iron bench with its back and seat made of ornate scrollwork of curly vines and leaves a la Art Nouveaux.

Yolanda didn't walk into the school right away but paused on the sidewalk and looked, beyond the fence and the front yard, at the Mansion as if she was seeing it for the very first time, even though she had spent almost the entire last year there. But then, as a student of the tutoring school, she had been a guest, and now, as a student of the proper school, she had arrived.

The Mansion was built in late nineteenth century, formal and austere, following a style that might be called neoclassic with a contemporary touch of the time. Its pitched roof, hiding behind tall parapets, was almost invisible from the ground. And the two-story and a half Mansion, with triangular pediments above the second floor windows, lofty paned windows on the second and first floors, small recessed windows on the half basement, quoins around the corners of its three rectangular building blocks with the center block bigger in area than the symmetrical east and west blocks, was covered by beige stucco and sat in the middle of the property like a giant beige mass, between two eight-foot high, beige-stuccoed masonry walls along the east and the west of the property,

Except the lawns in the front yard, the rest of the property (an area extended five-foot beyond the front of the Mansion, the twenty-five foot wide east and west side yards, and the sixty-foot deep back yard) was paved with concrete by the school.

And unlike the grand stair at the front, the other stairs to the Mansion were modest. The two narrow stairs in the side yards, one at the end of east building block and one at the end of west building block, that went up to first floor and down to basement; and the two five-foot wide stairs in the backyard, that rose to each end of a five-foot wide platform on first floor outside the back entrance to the Mansion; had cement sealed concrete steps and railings of plain black iron bars with simple scroll at the ends of the top rails as the only decorative feature.

And the structure across the back of the backyard was a crude building.

****

The center building block contained three halls; each hall was twenty-foot wide by sixty-foot long with the long side in the south-north direction. They were magnificent; the airy beige plaster, flamboyant chandeliers, and solemn dark mahogany, apparently the philanthropist's various architectural penchants put together, worked in harmony instead of against each other because of the simple way they were grouped. But they had lost their shine and looked dull, especially the floor of dark mahogany strips that was worn after years of tramping as the thoroughfare of the school.

The twelve-foot high main hall had beige plaster on the coved ceiling that extended four-foot down the wall to butt into a dark mahogany molding around the hall. Three beige plaster wreaths, molded into intricate curly leaves and flowers a la Art Nouveaux, lay evenly lengthwise across the middle of the ceiling. From the center of each wreath, copper chains spread out like an umbrella to hold the copper frame of a glittering chandelier of hundreds teardrop crystals.

Meeting the dark mahogany molding from below were eight-foot high dark mahogany wall panels. The wall panels were four-foot wide with one-foot wide fluted dark mahogany strips between them and at the four corners of the hall. The front entrance on the south and the back entrance on the north of the hall were paned dark mahogany double-doors of five-foot wide by seven-foot high, in one-foot wide fluted dark mahogany frames. On each side of each entrance there was a paned window that was three-foot wide by five-foot high with dark mahogany sill at three-foot above the floor. The two openings at the back of the hall, one on east wall to east hall and one on west wall to west hall, were three-foot wide, of the same height and in the same frame as the entrances. Like the wall panels; the entrances, the windows, and the openings also meet the dark mahogany molding at the top.

By the front entrance, in front of east wall, the school put up a bulky dark mahogany counter that matched the hall in weight and dignity. Across the counter, the school hung five aluminum display cases on west wall, over the dark mahogany panels, that were the commercial type with glass doors and built-in fluorescent strips. Neatly displayed and evenly illuminated in them were the school schedules, school notices, school news, and the like.

The east and west halls were symmetrical. The beige plaster on the coved ceiling also extended four-foot down the walls to butt into the dark mahogany molding around the halls, but the dark mahogany wall panels rose two-story in height, therefore the two halls were more stately than main hall. The front half of each hall was two-story in height with three two-story windows on the south facing the front yard; and the back half of each hall had six windows, three on first floor and three on second floor, on the north facing the backyard; therefore the two halls were also much brighter than main hall.

In the front half of each hall, under a wreath and a chandelier similar to those in main hall on the center of the soaring ceiling; an L-shaped, five-foot wide, dark mahogany stair rose, along the south wall and the wall next to main hall, to the second floor. The open side of the stair and the front of the second floor were guarded by heavy dark mahogany balustrade that had flutes carved on the four sides of its square banisters.

The seven doors and one opening in each hall were similar to those in main hall. Five of the doors were on the wall opposite the stair: two in the middle of the wall, one on first floor and one on second floor; two double-doors in the back half of the hall, one on first floor and one on second floor; and one double-door in the front half of the hall on first floor; these doors led from east hall to east building block and from west hall to west building block. On the dark mahogany closure around the underside of the stair on first floor, there was a locked door that led to the stair to the basement; behind this locked door, in the back half of the hall, was the opening to main hall; and above this opening, on second floor, was the door to the area above main hall.

Therefore, the area above main hall was accessed by two doors, one from east hall and one from west hall. In this area were the administrative offices and the office of the director of the school. In Yolanda's five years at the school, she had never seen the director, very few students had.

****

The east building block contained four bright and spacious classrooms, one in each area as the first and second floors were divided into two areas, the south area that faced the front yard and the north area that faced the backyard. Each area was twenty-foot wide by fifty-foot long with the long side in the east-west direction, and the five-foot wide corridor between them cut through the middle of each floor like a spine. On first floor, a door with opaque glass on the upper half, at the outer end of the corridor led to the stair in east side yard. As this door was locked, the classrooms were accessed from east hall only, by the door at the inner end of the corridor on both floors and by the double-doors in three of the four classrooms.

The symmetrical west building block contained various functions. On the second floor: the front portion of each area was a classroom, one of which was the tutoring school; the back portion of north area was the restrooms and of south area was a faculty room, none of the professors or instructors had an office at the school. And the entire first floor was the library.

The library was twelve-foot high and it was

the brightest, most pleasant, and best furnished place of the school. It had fluorescent lights in rows of off-white plastic cases on the coved ceiling of beige plaster, lofty windows lined on three sides of the walls that were also covered by beige plaster, and heavy dark mahogany furniture to match the sturdy floor of dark mahogany strips.

The corridor was opened up with six equally spaced openings on each side, as the corridor walls were structural walls that could not be removed in its entirety. The openings were three-foot wide by eight-foot high; lined between the openings and aligned at the top with them were eight-foot high dark mahogany book cases with hard covered volumes filed neatly on their open shelves; thus the corridor was turned into not only the connection between south and north areas but a stellar stack room as well.

The reading tables and chairs in south area that was the reading area; and the circulation counter, librarians' desks, catalogue cabinets, magazine racks and so forth in north area that was the circulation area; were grouped in the center of each area to free the space around the walls and the windows for circulation.

The only contemporary set was a coffee table with a large glass top and several easy chairs upholstered in bright colors around it, in north area near the entrance to the library that was the double-door to west hall. The double-door in south area to west hall and the door at each end of the corridor were locked.

****

But the center of school life was in the crude building in the back yard, where main curriculums like Architectural Design and City Planning took place. Courses like Building Structure, Construction Materials, and Architectural History were taught in the Mansion.

It was the only building built by the school. Its south front that looked out at the back of the Mansion across the backyard, was an aluminum curtain wall with windows on the upper half, solid panels on the lower half, and ten doors on it.

It had five studios in a row, one for each school year. Each studio was forty-two feet square in area. A square area this size free of interior columns was expensive to build at the time, but the studios were simply finished and furnished; the floor was bare concrete, the ceiling and the walls were covered by rough white plaster, the ceiling lighting fixtures at eight-foot long with exposed fluorescent tubes were the type used in factories, and the wood drafting tables and drafting stools, even though sturdy, were roughly constructed.

And with forty two drafting tables in each studio for forty students, the studios were jammed. The drafting tables with a top of three by five feet were arranged into six columns of seven drafting tables that ran parallel to the curtain wall, with five aisles in between that discharged at each end to a passage; the passage on the west led to the door at the west end of the curtain wall which was the front door, and the passage on the east led to the door at the east end of the curtain wall which was the back door. The aisles were only two-foot wide, often the students had to edge through; and the passages were only four-foot wide, as there was no room for a teacher's desk in front of west wall on which hung the blackboards, the drafting table next to the front door was kept free for the teachers to use.

Yet the crude studios were always splendid as sunlight shifted and changed colors in them, from warm golden in the morning, to dazzling yellow at noon, and intoxicating orange in the afternoon; and always vivid, brought to life by the high spirit of forty cheerful and forward looking young men and women in each studio.

Chapter II

Yolanda had never heard the word "architecture" back in China. Her family belonged to a clan of engineers. But after her father had moved the family to Brazil three years ago, her childhood dream of becoming an author was abruptly put to an end as she could only get by with Portuguese, the native language of Brazil. So after high school in Sao Paolo, she decided to study structure engineering as it was mostly calculations and drawings that she could manage without mastering the language, also as designing houses was what she liked second best after writing.

When she went to enroll for the entry exams at the School of Engineering and explained to the registration clerk what she wanted, the man said to her: "what you want is architecture, not structure engineering." And that was the very first time she ever heard the word "architecture".

She was sure that she would pass the architectural entry exams with ease. When she failed miserably, she was at first bitter, but soon she faced up to the fact that she knew nothing about architecture and enrolled in a tutoring school to prepare for next year's entry exams.

The architectural tutoring school was run by two men who had graduated from the School of Structural Engineering. They had been running the tutoring school for years as sideline business. They taught the engineering courses themselves and engaged an instructor from the School of Architecture to teach the architectural courses.

The School of Architecture graciously lent a classroom to the tutoring school for free. Thirty five tablet-chairs were packed into this small classroom; during break times, the boys would hurry off to walk up and down the corridor to bring circulation back to their numbed legs that had been tucked in the tight space under the tablet for a long time. Yet all the courses, including architectural design and drafting, were taught in this small room, and the students didn't mind the poor setting. Almost all of them had failed the previous entry exams and there was only one thing on their minds now: to pass the next entry exams. They studied with almost desperate zeal.

There were so many subjects to cover in nine months. School started at eight o'clock in the morning and ended at six in the evening, six days a week. Yolanda studied hard with the dread of failing the entry exams again looming in her mind. She kept mostly to herself, she hardly knew who the other students in the classroom were except that most of them were boys, only a few girls.

Time flew in this hectic pace, before Yolanda knew, October had come and the tutoring school was to wrap up at the end of the month.

The last school day was a Saturday and it was just like any other school day except at the end of the day the instructor said a few encouraging words to the students and wished everybody good luck, and the students packed up their things to hurry home like they had done at the end of all the other school days.

Yolanda was in no hurry to go home today. She felt relieved that the tutoring school was over but anxious at the same time that the entry exams were drawing that much nearer.

She walked down the stately stair in west hall slowly and absent-minded, as other students rushed down the stair around her. She was more than half way down the stair when, as if pulled by a magnet, she looked back and saw a tall boy on second floor, standing at the top of the stair. She recognized him as one of the students of the tutoring school who always took the chair in the inner back corner of the classroom.

He was staring at her. Suddenly the door across swung wide open and several students of the tutoring school burst out from the corridor and rushed for the stair. They bumped on him as they tramped down the stair in a hurry, but he didn't budge, he just stood there staring at her. The diffused light from the ebbing sun slanted in through the soaring windows on the south and shone on his delicate face, and Yolanda saw he had boyish pale blue eyes which were now flooded with fascination.

Chapter III

Yolanda walked into the front yard through the gate, the paired leaves of which were swung fully open inward. She walked quickly over the gigantic tree shadows on the footpath, toward the Mansion that was basking in golden sunshine. A group of students in the shade of a tree: two young women sitting in the Art Nouveaux bench and three young men standing around them, stopped talking when she passed and cast casual glances at her, she didn't look at them. A student who came from behind said hello to her as he overtook her, she didn't return the courtesy.

The chandeliers in main hall were not turned on, the back of the long hall seemed far, far away and was dim in daylight that filtered in through the two open windows flanking the closed back entrance. In contrast, the front of the hall was bright in sunlight that cast three elongated golden patches on the floor through the open front entrance and the two open windows flanking it.

She greeted the middle aged and medium height school keeper, who was sitting behind the bulky dark mahogany counter, with the formal and distant nod that she had greeted him for the past year; she rarely talked to him except for school information, she was not good at small talks and didn't think it was necessary.

Then she proceeded quickly to the back toward the opening to east hall, she needed to go to the administrative office before class. Unlike the main hall, the east hall was dazzling in light, in daylight from the six windows at the back and in sunlight from the three soaring windows at the front.

As she was walking up the stair, the door from the administrative office flung open and someone jumped out, it was the tall and handsome boy. At seeing Yolanda, he stopped abruptly and was taken aback, apparently he didn't expect seeing her here, but then his pale blue eyes brightened up. He ran down the stair without looking at her, without saying hello. He passed her so swiftly that she turned sideways to let him by.

When she resumed her way up, she thought to herself: "so he got in also."

Chapter IV

Yolanda's family was well-off in China. She studied at the best schools where she was happy, her teachers and classmates appreciated her for her literary talent and her straight character. But she was an unappreciated child at home, her family didn't think much of her, to them she was not clever enough and too stubborn. She never had a doll to hold and to play with when a little girl and was never dressed prettily like her cousins. When she was seven years old, she started to stutter and every time she did, her relatives and her family laughed at her in amusement. She could probably have overcome all these, had she not been molested by a relative when she was eleven years old.

She became aware that she was a beautiful girl when she was fifteen in Taiwan where her family lived for a year after they had left mainland China and before they moved to Brazil. Being a naïve girl, she wasn't aware of it for quite sometime, but in time the stealthy glances the boys at school cast at her awaked her instinct.

And she had been dreamt about love ever since, the kind of noble and undying love like in the Chinese and western (which she read in Chinese translation) classic novels. And ever since she had been in love in secret, first in Taiwan and then in Brazil, at various times with various boys at school, who had caught her heart by falling in love with her also in secret.

But it was in Brazil she came of age and people stared at her because of her beauty. It was also in Brazil she started to dress herself not as austerely as in China.

Her aura was noble and intense. Under pencil straight black eyebrows, double eyelids and black eyelashes, in large snow white eyes, her brown eye balls and black pupils were so captivating that many people, both men and women, felt uneasy looking at her. She had fine and lustrous black hair, ivory smooth skin on her oblong face, pinkish high cheekbones, a straight nose, tight red lips, neat teeth, and square jaws. She was five-foot and four-inch tall and youthfully slim, but her chest was almost as flat as a boy's.

Her world changed in Brazil. There were only several hundred Chinese in Sao Paolo at the time, almost all of them came recently like Yolanda's family to escape the communist regime that had just taken over China. In this small community, Yolanda found herself among Chinese who were full of jealousy and intrigue, but in the bigger outside world, the Brazilians were simpler and warmer. Suddenly she stopped stutter.

But she had become a complex person. Men of poor wits mistook her as being timid and easy to maneuver, only to keep away from her with disgust when they saw her disturbed soul in display. In such occasions, she would lose her temper and argue heatedly, even with strangers, as if to let out the rage in her.

Chapter V

Most of the students of the first year class had been students at the tutoring school and Yolanda was not surprised to see the tall and handsome boy among them as she had run into him outside the administrative office on the first school day.

Soon after school had started, the school gave a Sunday outing at a country club as a getting acquainted party for the new and old students. Every one of the first year class attended with much enthusiasm.

As the day started to wane in late afternoon, Yolanda and several girls of her class sat around a table by the swimming pool. The girls were chatting and watching the boys who formed a long line at the foot of a diving tower at the other end of the huge swimming pool, waiting for their turn to dive. In the presence of the girls, they made much noise, talking and laughing, and when it came to their turn to dive, they plunged into the water with so much force to show off that water shot up all around them.

Yolanda was not watching the boys, her mind was elsewhere. The crimson sun shone on her fascinating face and the jade luster of the wavering water in the swimming pool reflected on her loose white cotton dress and her bare feet. Suddenly her mind was pulled back to the present and, as if forced by a magnet, she looked upward toward the diving tower and saw the tall and handsome boy.

He was standing near the tip of the diving board, ready to dive, but instead he stood there staring at her. So far away and so high above was he and with the setting sun behind him, she could not see his features distinctly except his pale blue eyes, they were very clear as he stared at her.

He stood there staring at her until the boy behind him came up to him and cried out: "Wake up! Enrique," and pushed him into the water, the other boys roared with laughter, when Enrique stuck his head above the water, they laughed even louder; he looked around with a boyish shy air and blushed, looking bewildered but radiantly happy.

He had been a vague impression in Yolanda's mind ever since she saw him staring at her from the top of the stair on the last tutoring school day. Now his image was imprinted vividly on her mind.

She went home that night ecstatically in love. Enrique had caught her passionate young heart with his passionate young eyes.

Chapter VI

Enrique de Manza, like Yolanda, was twenty years old. Despite his boyish aura, he was poised and composed. He was tall and slim but not thin, had fine sandy hair and fine complexion, a delicate face and intelligent pale blue eyes. From his looks, Yolanda thought he was of German descendant; actually his family was member of a prominent Italian clan in Sao Paulo.

But his father had died when he was eight years old, now he had only his mother and a kid sister who was eight years his junior and who had never seen their father.

He dressed simply; during the five school years, he wore only white shirts, narrow black ties, black pants, dark socks and wide toed black shoes. The only change was his suit coats, for the first three years he wore a light brown ruggedly woven suit coat and for the last two years, a pale green ruggedly woven suit coat. But he was neat and clean, and his clothes were meticulously pressed. Yolanda thought he was the best dressed among the boys of the class.

He had two best friends in the class. He, Arturo, and Roberto did everything together. They went to tutoring school together and Yolanda had the feeling they had known each other long before that, all three showed the same poise and good breeding.

Yet they were actually very different. In height, Enrique at six feet was the tall one, Arturo in the middle, and Roberto the short and wide one. In looks, Enrique was handsome, Arturo strikingly good looking, and Roberto macho. In temperament, Enrique was boyish, Arturo the play boy, and Roberto serious.

And only Enrique had a frequent visitor at school. His cousin Viola often came to visit him in the afternoon during the architectural design sessions.

Yolanda had seen Viola at the tutoring school, she attended it briefly and dropped out shortly, Yolanda heard that she wasn't up to the study.

She was a year younger than Enrique, tall, thin, brunette, plain looking, but very poised. She wore her hair straight at shoulder length, dark colored dresses, black stockings, flat black shoes, and a string of several thin silver bangles around her left wrist. Yolanda had the strange feeling that she was the perfect match for Enrique.

When she came to visit him, she would stand by his drafting table, watching him working; passing pencils, erasers, rulers and other drafting tools to him as he needed them. She was friendly with Arturo and Roberto, and also with some other students of the class.

They also came together to the school parties that took place in main hall on the first Saturday night of every month. They stayed together throughout the party, dancing with no one but each other.

Yolanda didn't mind Viola, she could tell Enrique's feeling for her was innocent.

Chapter VII

Among the forty first year students, only eight were girls and by the fifth school year all of them were engaged, either to a classmate, a schoolmate, or a student at the School of Engineering, except Yolanda and Maria, a good natured and slightly overweight girl.

When Belinda was still at tutoring school, Alfredo, a mature and self-assured third year architectural student at the time, had set eyes on her, and they soon went steady. Belinda was a brunette with large eyes, she took great care of her looks, dressed well and was always presentable. She was conscious of her beauty and a little vain, she had her ways with the boys and was very popular among them, for this Yolanda was jealous of her, even thought she was genuinely nice and kind to Yolanda. And she was very intelligent and very mature for a young woman only twenty years of age, she seemed to have sailed through the five school years doing nothing but happily dating Alfredo, yet she got good grades on all subjects. Alfredo had been doing well as a young architect since graduation, and they were to marry as soon as she graduated. Belinda spent the last school year happily preparing for her wedding, her eyes showed the fulfillment of a young woman in love and who had her dreams come true.

Eliza was of the class a year junior to Yolanda's, but she came to Yolanda's studio often after she became Umberto's girl friend in her third school year. Umberto was Yolanda's classmate, good looking, of medium height and well bred, but Yolanda never noticed him until she noticed Eliza. Eliza was tall and attractive, she was equally nice to girls and boys, her attitude didn't take the subtle change, like the other girls, when boys were around; and she didn't hide her feelings from Umberto, while the other girls were consistently sweet in front of their boy friends. One day, Yolanda saw her running out of the studio, red faced with anger, with Umberto running after her, calling: "Eliza, wait. Wait!" Yolanda was impressed by her independent character, maybe that was why Umberto, genteel and mild, was so crazy about her.

Alicia, at eighteen, was the youngest student in Yolanda's class, where the average age was twenty, and the brightest. She was the number one student of all subjects, which Yolanda resented, for Yolanda thought herself excellent in architecture design and structure engineering. But Alicia was not a bookworm and didn't wear glasses, far from it, she was pretty and sweet looking with innocent large brown eyes, yet she didn't have a boy friend until the fifth school year. Federico was of the class a year senior to

Alicia's and five years her senior in age. He carried a rebellious air and when he came to the school parties, he came with a different high school girl each time. But after he had graduated, he seriously courted Alicia, they soon went steady and Alicia was as happy as a little bird. When she got a scholarship for postgraduate study in Italy, after having made sure two people could live modestly in Italy with her scholarship, they decided to marry after her graduation and go to Italy together. It was an odd match, Federico's rebellious air might very well be the cover up of an unsure young man; and the level headed and intelligent Alicia, despite being that much younger than Federico in age, might actually be more mature and stronger.

Even Carla had Washington for a boy friend. Carla wore her hair short like a boy, she was tall, ugly, and proud, and she detested Yolanda; she never looked at Yolanda, every time Yolanda happened to be near her, she would swivel her head to look the other way with contempt in her eyes, and Yolanda, being negligent by nature, didn't pay attention to her. Washington was heavy and stupid, still a student at the School of Engineering in his mid-thirties, but Carla treated him as if he was the most fabulous man on earth. When he came to visit her in the studio, she would bend her knees so that she would be at the same height as he, put her arms around his shoulders, and gaze at him with worshipping eyes. It was obvious that she was very proud of herself for being able to catch a man at all. Their marriage was a sure thing, their families had known each other for generations.

Chapter VIII

The curriculums of the first school year were classes in the morning that took place in the Mansion and architectural design session in the afternoon that took place in the studio. In this simple life and setting, the students soon felt very much at home.

Each student chose a drafting table in the studio that was to be his or hers for the next five school years, Yolanda chose one at the front of the studio, and Enrique chose one at the back next to Arturo and Roberto's. The desks in the classrooms were not assigned, and Yolanda always sat in the front of the classroom and Enrique in the back with Arturo and Roberto.

Yolanda could feel Enrique watching her from his seat whether in the studio or in the classrooms, and when she looked back, she would meet his eyes, he didn't try to look away to avoid her, he kept staring at her, unabashedly like a happy little boy.

Soon she also realized he followed her around the school, wherever she happened to be, he would show up shortly after. When she was in the library, heaping up a reading table with books and magazines, ready to spend a comfortable afternoon in the wonderful world of reading, he would appear and walk around her reading table just once, without saying a word to her, before leaving the library as quietly as he had come. While she was having lunch, at noon every day, in the little food shed in west side yard, he would pop his head in at the door, take a quick look of her like a mischievous little boy, then retreat and disappear from the side yard. Soon she began to expect his presence where ever she happened to be.

One sunny morning, she was sitting in the front yard, on the Art Nouveaux bench under a tree, with Maria and Dora who was Maria's best friend, when Enrique emerged from the Mansion with Arturo and Roberto. At the sight of her, his face brightened up like the morning sun, and as he walked past her, he cast a quick glance at her that revealed his enormous feeling for her. Yolanda was ecstatic.

The architectural design assignment was for each of the new students to design his or her dream house, a most proper first assignment for the future architects, for each of them already had one in mind, and now they strove to put it on drawings.

One afternoon Viola, who had made acquaintance with Yolanda, brought a paperboard, on which was the perspective drawing of Enrique's dream house, to

Yolanda's drafting table. Viola couldn't hide her enthusiasm and acclaimed: "isn't it wonderful!" But Yolanda only took a casual look at the drawing and said nothing, she was surprised and happy at this unexpected gesture, but she was too shy to know what to say. To her, everything Enrique did was good without saying, she believed in his talent just like she believed in his love for her, and was sure he knew how she felt; she was only disappointed that he didn't bring the drawing himself to show her. When Viola took the drawing back to Enrique, she couldn't hide her discouragement.

But when the second semester came, Viola didn't come to visit Enrique at school anymore and she also stopped coming to the school parties with him. Now Enrique came alone and stayed out the party with Arturo and Robert; the three of them would stand by the dancing floor, chatting and watching the dancing crowd, except when Arturo went away to dance with some pretty girl, then Enrique and Roberto would stand together, chatting and watching.

Yolanda always came to the parties by a ride from her father and spent most of the time alone, while she was dying to dance and to have fun. As beautiful as she was, she was not popular. Now she was dying for Enrique to ask her to dance, but he never did; he didn't even look at her at the parties.

Chapter IX

When the second school year came, as Yolanda's class watched the enthusiasm of the first year newcomers, a feeling they only knew too well, they could hardly believe they themselves were not newcomers any more.

But all this had no bearing with Yolanda, she was too wrapped in her own happiness, Enrique followed her around the school like always.

So she felt lost one afternoon, when she went to the library and Enrique didn't show up. She did not stay long in the library and started to go back to the studio; just as she was in west hall getting to main hall, the back entrance in main hall was thrust wide open, daylight rushed into main hall through the double-door and rushed in together with daylight was a group of noisy students, among them Belinda, Alfredo, Arturo, Roberto, and Enrique. They were all talking, laughing, and gesturing at the same time, except for a quiet girl beside Enrique. She was about thirteen or fourteen years of age, still growing but already tall, had large brown eyes on her delicate face, her brunette hair was cut short to the ears, and she wore the catholic girl school's austere uniform of white shirt, black tie, black jacket, black skirt, black stockings, and laced black shoes. She looked timid beside the group of "spunky adults", and hesitated at the doorway. Enrique stopped with her while the others stepped briskly into main hall; he looked down at her gently and nudged her elbow lightly to urge her in. Yolanda was moved by this scene and was happy that

Enrique was a loving and protective big brother to his kid sister.

The architectural design assignment for the second school year was an apartment building, and the students had the choice of working alone or as a group. Yolanda worked alone on a small apartment building; Enrique, Arturo and Roberto worked together on one of large scale.

T-square was the basic drafting tool for architectural students and everyone in Yolanda's class had one except her and Maria. Yolanda didn't know why Maria didn't have one; as for her, it wasn't that she couldn't afford one, but rather that she could get by without one. Eventually she and Maria both got a T-square later, but for now she was doing fine with triangles and rulers only, so she didn't bother to buy one.

One afternoon, during the architectural design session in the studio, she was so absorbed working on her apartment project that she lost the count of time, when she finally raised her head to take a break, she saw Enrique by her drafting table. He must have been standing there for sometime and he was looking at her quietly; her black hair was cut short to the ears and combed into soft large waves, her red lips were only slightly touched by lipstick, and she wore a long-sleeved grayish-blue acrylic pullover, a light wool full skirt of the same color, nylon stockings, and grey suede pumps. She looked at him with the concentrated air still on her face, he blushed when their eyes met, but said to her in a poised voice: "you can use my T-square."

Without expecting it, Yolanda's wish had come true, Enrique came to talk to her in person. She was so happy but she merely looked at him, for she didn't know what to say to him, she had never had a boy she liked talking to her, and he didn't talk to her the way she expected. She expected a dashing declaration of love like in the novels, "you can use my T-square" was so ordinary and so like every-day talk; she failed to see the effort behind this gesture. She said nothing while waiting for him to carry the conversation further, but he said nothing more, he blushed deeper as he walked away, leaving her feeling abandoned. But she didn't show her emotion, she went back to work on her apartment project as if nothing had happened.

And she didn't go to him to borrow his T-square, the thought had never crossed her mind. Not only that, she now acted as if she wanted to avoid not only him but also his friends, while she longed for him to talk to her again. He didn't even come near her for the rest of the semester.

When he approached her again, it was already in the second semester and near the end of the school year. This time he did it with subtlety, without the directness of the T-square episode.

Yolanda and Maria took the electric car at the back of the school to go home everyday. One afternoon, in early November, as the electric car was about to start, someone jumped aboard and it was Enrique. Yolanda had not seen him at the bus stop, he must have been hidden from them on purpose. It was now late spring and the weather was getting warm, but at after five o'clock in the afternoon, it was cool inside the electric car, as air flowed freely to and fro in the open cabin. The ebbing sun shone on Yolanda's lovely face and her cloth; she wore a short-sleeved white cotton shirt buttoned up to the neck, a canary-yellow cotton skirt seamed together with six tapered pieces, nylon stockings, and wide-toed dark brown pumps on one-inch stacked heels. Enrique took a seat facing her across the aisle, nodded to her and said hello. Yolanda's heart began to pound wildly with happiness, Enrique was following her! She knew he didn't live in this direction and had never seen him in this electric car. Yet she didn't return the courtesy but waited for him to move over to sit by her and start a conversation. He didn't, he remained where he was, and when he got off two stops later, he didn't even look at her, leaving her feeling abandoned.

Yolanda spent the long summer vacation dreaming about marrying Enrique and becoming prominent architects together.

Chapter X

When the third school year came, Yolanda's class had felt completely old hands at school. This year they became big brothers and sisters of the first year new comers, a role they carried out with ease.

Still all this had no bearing with Yolanda. She was now so in love with Enrique that every time he was near her, she became even more beautiful, while ignoring him like always. Her emotion did not escape the other girls' shrewd eyes, those who liked her couldn't understand her, and those who disliked her thought she was hatefully pretentious by playing hard to get.

But Enrique had stopped following her around the school. He still sort of following her with his eyes, when she looked back at him in the studio, she would see him at his drafting table, staring at her and yet not staring at her, mostly he was staring into the air. He looked pensive and perplexed, his pale blue eyes were clouded now. Yolanda saw the change, but she thought it was nothing.

And Enrique, Arturo, and Roberto had gone their separate ways, they were still together sometimes, but no longer doing everything together like before. The architectural design assignment for this school year was a public building; Yolanda chose to design a small post office, perhaps because she was impressed with the magnificent neoclassic post office building, by the enormous plaza in front of which she transferred everyday from the bus she took at home to the electric car she took to school. She didn't know what kind of public building Enrique was designing, but this year he worked alone.

Yolanda didn't have any friend at school. She spent much time with Maria and Dora, not because she enjoyed their company, she found them dull, but because she had to be with someone, and the three of them were the only girls in the class who didn't have a boy friend. Later when Dora became the girl friend of a classmate, Maria and Yolanda were together a lot, even though Dora remained Maria's best friend. Dora didn't care about Yolanda, she went along with her because of Maria.

Yolanda argued a lot with Paolo, as she had a penchant to argue with people, and Paolo's drafting table was conveniently next to hers, but she didn't consider him her friend, nor did he consider himself hers. Paolo was skinny and bright, and Yolanda was comfortable with him because he was like a harmless kid brother. He was excellent in Calculus in the first school year, Building Dynamics in the second, and Structure Design in the third, so Yolanda loved to argue about all three subjects with him. Sometimes she became so heated in those arguments, that her face turned red and her eyes bloodshot, as she was so convinced she was right, while she was wrong.

Yolanda didn't consider the "Count" her friend either, even though she started flirting with him during the third school year. The "Count" was a true count from Italy, in his late twenties, therefore was considered an "old fellow" by the class. He was short but wide built, had big features on a big face: large eyes, big nose and broad lips. She called him "Count" and teased him all the time, and he good naturedly like a gentleman, let her flirt with him while he never talked to her on his own. Many classmates thought she was trying to catch the "Count"; had she known what was on people's mind, she would have felt deeply offended; she would not even try to catch Enrique, much less the dull "Count". She flirted with him because she didn't care a bit about him and knew he felt the same way about her; she felt lousy every time she flirted with him, but she couldn't stop herself. She was sure Enrique knew it was all innocent, just like she knew his feeling for Viola was innocent.

Yolanda spent the third school year in discontent and unrest. Toward the end of the school year in November, a storm was suddenly gathering one afternoon at about three o'clock. The sun disappeared and the bright sky turned gloomy instantly, followed by splitting lightening and rolling thundering. The rain came half an hour later, first in large and sparse drops hitting hard against the concrete pavement in the backyard, before it started to pour.

By then everybody had gone home, by a ride from either a classmate or a schoolmate, Yolanda was the only one left in the studio. Enrique was nowhere to be seen.

From the bright studio lit by fluorescent lights, she watched impatiently, through the curtain wall windows, the rain pouring in the gloomy backyard, waiting for it to die down. When it finally did at five o'clock, she hopped across the backyard over the puddles of rain for main hall.

The long hall was gloomy and deserted except for the school keeper, who was sitting behind the bulky dark mahogany counter. Suddenly an urgent urge for Enrique engulfed her and she stared into the dark opening to west hall, hoping he would hop through it from the library, knowing it was unlikely. Indeed only the dark opening stared back at her in mocking silence.

She stood inside the front entrance, side by side with the school keeper, watching the rain that had started pouring again. The misty sky hung low as the rain poured incessantly, soaking the old mansions yonder, the street, the sidewalk, the fence, the lawns, the trees, the Art Nouveaux benches, the footpath, the stair, and the platform just outside the front entrance.

She arrived home at about nine o'clock that evening. The rain had stopped but she was soaking wet. Her parents and siblings were in the living room watching TV as usual, and they looked at her but said nothing as she passed them on the way to her room. When she closed the door behind her in her room, she felt utterly alone in the world.

Chapter XI

There was a big change in curriculum for the fourth school year, city planning was added, and the students often spent the entire day in the studio alternately with city planning and architectural design.

Yolanda's spirit revived at seeing Enrique again after the long summer vacation, despite the change of his attitude toward her.

But two months into the first semester, something very sad happened, Enrique's mother died. Now he and his kid sister were left alone in the world. Yolanda learnt of the sad news rather late by overhearing two classmates talking about it, no one told her. Enrique was absent from school for two weeks, and when he came back, he was thin and pale, and wore a black crepe band around the left arm of his pale green ruggedly woven suit coat.

Yolanda's heart went out to him, but she acted with her usual nonchalance, and didn't even offer him condolence as common courtesy, she had shown more sympathy when Dora's mother died. Even an event as devastating as this one couldn't bring her out of her shell to show her emotion, yet she was sure Enrique knew how she felt, and to her things went back to normal soon enough, despite that now he had stopped looking at her altogether.

In fact he had vanished from school. He always came to the studio by the back door, and Yolanda would know he had come by feeling him stare at her from his drafting table. Now when she couldn't resist the urge to look back, she only saw his empty drafting table. She missed him terribly and that did not escape the sharp eyed girls; those who liked her felt sorry for her, and those who disliked her were devilishly delighted that she had finally got what she deserved.

When Yolanda did see Enrique again, it wasn't at school. Near the end of May, a classmate invited the entire class for a Saturday outing at his parents' beach house. Yolanda spent the day with Maria, feeling low. She didn't expect to see Enrique, but in the afternoon, there he was, standing at the end of the hallway by the study, talking to the host; a small over-night bag lay on the floor by his feet. His face was fuller and he looked in peace, the black crepe band on the sleeve was gone. He didn't look at Yolanda, even though she was in full view, standing with Maria at the other end of the hallway by the living room; he acted as if she was not there. She heard him saying to the host with boyish earnest: "Ask Arturo to stay for the night too, he would love to."

Yolanda suddenly remembered another outing where, by the intoxicating ebbing sun of a beautiful late summer afternoon, a handsome and boyish young man was staring at her, from the tip of a diving tower above a gigantic swimming pool, with so much fascination in his eloquent eyes. How happy they were then and it didn't seem long ago, but three and a half years had passed.

Before the first semester ended, Yolanda saw Enrique one more time, at the last school party of the semester. As always she came to the party alone and didn't expect to see him at the party, he had not come back to school after the beach house outing. When the party was well in advance, a dull and middle-aged man, whom Yolanda had never seen before, invited her to take a walk in the courtyard, and when they returned to main hall, the man vanished. Yolanda stood by the dancing floor, watching the dancing crowd, and she saw Enrique and Viola. They were at the other end of the dim hall, he held her tightly in his arms with her back to Yolanda; they were not really dancing, only swaying on the same spot following the rhythm of a slow fox-trot. It was Enrique's stare that attracted Yolanda's attention to them; he was staring at her across the long hall, with intense hatred in his eyes. Yet Yolanda's spirit soared, Enrique was staring at her again, everything was just like before! She didn't think it was much that he came to the party with Viola, he had come to the parties with her before, she didn't see that before they had come as cousins, now they came as lovers.

So when the second semester started and the whole school was talking about Enrique's coming marriage with Viola, she was shocked beyond belief. She heard Carla saying with relief: "poor Enrique, he had suffered so," as if she was glad that his misery was finally over.

Yolanda's emotion was boiling, Enrique could not marry any one! He loved her and love was forever! Enrique had come back to school this semester and she confronted him one afternoon, before a lecture on Building Materials was about to start. The large classroom in the south area on second floor of east building block could hardly hold all the bright sunshine in it. She suddenly left her desk at the front and found herself by his desk at the back, and she cried out: "I thought you loved me!" It was the only time she talked to him, truly talked to him, revealing her raw emotion. He was taken aback and they looked at each other eye to eye with rage, his retort was sharp and short: "I never loved you!" The classroom that had been humming with students' chatting, fell into deadly silence all at once. Yolanda didn't know how she got back to her desk, but when the lecturer arrived five minutes later, the class had resumed the humming as if nothing had happened.

Yolanda didn't feel embarrassed or humiliated, there was no room in her blunt personality for such nonsense. And she didn't care that she made a big fool of herself in front of every body, she was never one to bother much with what others think of her. She could not believe it could end like this, and so sudden and so final. She never expected such ruthless denial from him. But afterwards, when she cooled off, and with fairness, she admitted he was right, there had never been anything between them beyond fascination from a distance. Still, didn't the way they felt about each other, justify her feeling betrayed and poignantly hurt?

After the classroom confrontation, Enrique vanished from school again, but that didn't concern Yolanda anymore, he was out of her life forever.

Enrique and Viola married during the summer vacation. One day Yolanda saw Viola's picture in the wedding section of the newspaper. She wore a simple wedding gown, her face behind a trailing bridal veil, and she was standing beside a middle-aged man, who must be her father, with her arm in his; there was a brief wedding announcement below the picture. It didn't stir Yolanda a bit, it was expected.

Chapter XII

The curriculum for the fifth school year was very much like the fourth, emphasizing architectural design and city planning, except that the teachers did very little instruction now, mostly they acted as advisors to the students.

And Yolanda's dream of becoming a prominent architect was what kept her going, besides this, she felt alienated from school, she didn't feel she belonged any more. She stopped arguing with Paolo and could discuss things calmly with him now. As for the "Count", she stopped talking to him altogether.

Three boys in her class showed their interests in her, but they retreated quickly as she ignored them completely.

Enrique only came to school for the architectural design sessions this semester, he had dropped all other subjects. He still wore the pale green ruggedly woven suit coat and there was a simple golden wedding ring on his finger.

Now Yolanda sometimes went to the back of the studio to look at the students' design drawings posted on east wall. She could not have brought herself to be near there before, because of her feelings for Enrique.

One afternoon she wandered to there to do just that, without realizing there were only she, Enrique, and Carla in the studio, until she heard Carla saying, behind her back, jokingly to Enrique: "poor Enrique, Viola kept you wait twenty minutes for her at the wedding."

It immediately struck Yolanda that Carla was saying this for her to hear. Carla must have thought she didn't know Enrique had married, and she came to the back of the studio, pretending looking at the drawings, as her scheme to be near him. She felt disgusted and stopped going there thereafter. She was surprised at how quickly she grasped Carla's mean mind, she had matured and she missed immensely the happy old days when she was silly and naïve.

At the beginning of June, as the first semester was nearing the end, Yolanda was working on her architectural project, which was an assembly building for this school year and she chose to design a small theater, in the studio one morning without distraction, when someone squeezed on her back. How dare anyone be so fresh! She flung her head in fury to see who it was and saw Enrique, he was on his way from his drafting table at the back to the curtain wall windows at the front, by squeezing his way through the narrow space between Yolanda's row of drafting tables and the row behind. Only then, did Yolanda realize it was noontime and everybody had gone to lunch, she and Enrique were the only two people in the sunshine bright studio. When she saw it was he, strangely her fury was gone and she was devoid of feelings. She said and did nothing.

He had already squeezed his way passed her, and was now at the windows, looking out to the backyard. He was blushing when he went back to his drafting table, this time by way of the west passage and an aisle. He had barely sat down at his drafting table, when a classmate, who seemed to have appeared in the backyard from nowhere, stuck his head in at the front door and shouted sharply to him: "Viola is here!" and disappeared from the backyard as quickly as he had appeared.

Then Yolanda saw Viola, she had just emerged from the back entrance to the Mansion and was coming down to the backyard. She stopped midway on the stair, stooped and looked into the studio through the curtain wall windows.

She did not change much from the last time Yolanda had seen her a year ago at the school party, still wore flat shoes and the string of thin silver bangles on her left wrist, and she wore a white collared loose black maternity dress with printed tiny white flowers on it.

Enrique walked quickly out of the studio to meet her in the backyard, together they walked up the stair again and vanished into the back entrance. On his way out, he didn't look at Yolanda, he acted as if there was no one in the studio but him.

That was the last time Yolanda saw Enrique. He did not come to school thereafter. Yolanda thought he would come back for the second semester, but he didn't, another student took his drafting table. Yolanda was dying to know what had happened, but she couldn't ask anyone. Apparently he had dropped the entire fifth school year to come back next year.

And Yolanda had much to occupy her time and her mind now. Her father, concerned she didn't have a boy friend, was sending her to study at graduate school in America, hoping she would find a husband among the Chinese students, who came from Taiwan and Hong Kong to study at American universities for advanced degrees. Finding a husband was not in Yolanda's mind, but going to study in America was a big thrill.

After she had asked the administrative office to transfer her school credentials to the American universities to which she was applying for admission, the entire class knew she was going to America, but no one asked her about it. When she told Paolo and Dora about it, they showed polite disinterest, only Maria wished her good luck and they promised to write each other, but never did.

School finished in November, Yolanda left for America in December, with an empty heart, without attending the graduation ceremony and the graduation party that were to take place in January.

Chapter XIII

Yolanda would eventually live happily; for the urge to live and to live happily in her was stronger than love, even obsessed love.

Years later, when she truly matured and became a person of open mind and kind heart in America, she wondered had Enrique truly loved her, or only desired her? Or one and the other are really the same, or one could turn into the other, when love turned sour.

Why did he squeeze her back that day? Had she known he could behave like that, would she still have loved him? The young man she loved was pure and passionate, not sneaky and obscene. Why did he do it? To provoke her to make another scene, this time in front of Viola; because like Carla, he also believed going to the back of the studio, looking at the drawings, was her scheme to be near him?

The only thing she was sure was that her absurd behavior made a mess of everything, and did so much harm to Enrique and to herself. Otherwise two people who feel the way they had felt about each other will naturally get together, and whatever the outcome, she would not have to carry the regret for the rest of her life that she had a dream and she missed the chance to live it.

The End

Printed in the United States
142115LV00001B/14/P